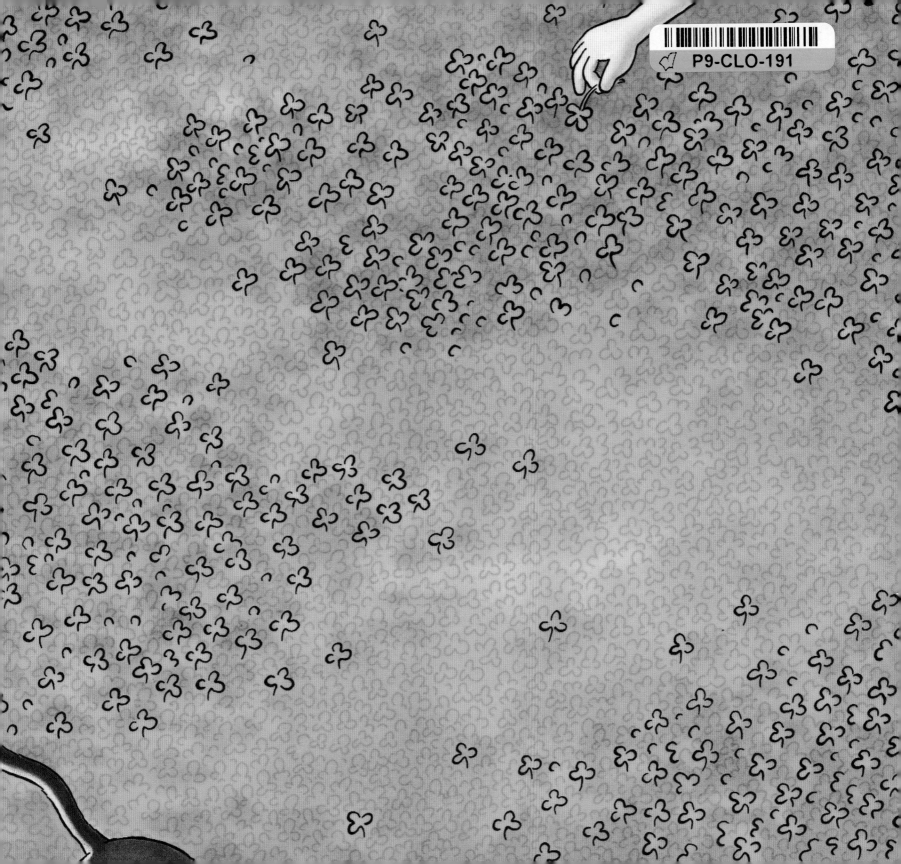

Library of Congress Cataloging-in-Publication Data · Ernst, Lisa Campbell · The luckiest kid on the planet / by Lisa Campbell Ernst. — 1st ed. p. cm. Summary: When he learns that Lucky is not his real name, but only a nickname given to him by his grandfather, a young boy's outlook on his whole life changes. ISBN 0-02-733566-6 [1. Grandfathers-Fiction. 2.Luck-Fiction. 3.Self-perception-Fiction.] I.Title. PZ7. E7323 Lu 1994 [Fic.] — dc20 93-36329

Bradbury Press. Macmillan Publishing Company. 866 Third Avenue New York, NY 10022. Maxwell Macmillan Canada Inc. 1200 Eglinton Avenue East · Suite 200 Don Mills, Ontario. M3C3N1. Macmillan Publishing Company is a part of the Maxwell Communications Group of Companies. First edition - Printed in Singapore on recycled paper by Toppan Printing Company. 10 9 8 7 6 5 4 3 2 1 The text of this book is set in Goudy Old Style. The illustrations are rendered in pastel, ink, and pencil. Special thanks to Lee and Elizabeth ♥

in memory of Ken and James

The LUCKIEST KID on the PLANET

LISA CAMPBELL ERNST

Bradbury Press   New York

Maxwell Macmillan Canada   Toronto
Maxwell Macmillan International
New York   Oxford   Singapore   Sydney

Lucky Morgenstern knew he was the world's luckiest kid.
How could he be anything else, with such a great name?

From the top of his head down to his socks, Lucky felt just that—lucky.

All around him, life was wonderful. The grass grew, flowers bloomed, stars twinkled. His parents, his hamster, even his little sister were wonderful. And best of all was his grandfather: They were best friends.

"Lucky, my boy," Grandfather would chuckle, "*you* are the luckiest kid on the planet!" And Lucky was quick to agree.

Every morning, Lucky woke up saying,
"I wonder what lucky things will happen today?"
If the sun shone, he said, "Lucky me, the sun
is shining." If it was raining, he said,
"Lucky me, I have an umbrella."

If he caught a
fish when he and his
grandfather went fishing,

or won when they played checkers,
Lucky knew it was because he was named Lucky.

If he made a great drawing,

or he found a rock
for his collection,

or his grandfather baked cookies,
it was because he was Lucky.

If his
hamster ran away
but his grandfather caught it,

or if he got to
ride his scooter
all day long—
if his best Razzmatazz-Red
crayon had been lost for two whole
months and his grandfather found it—
Lucky knew it was because he was Lucky.

Razzmatazz-Red

And all of his friends knew it, too.

Everyone wanted to sit next to him, talk to him, even borrow his socks—hoping some of that luck just might rub off on them.

Lucky pitied his friends, who all had ordinary names. "Sure, I have plenty of luck to spread around!" he boasted.

Let's face it, this boy was about to burst at the seams with luck.

"*You*," his grandfather was always there to agree, "are indeed the luckiest kid on the planet."

But then one fateful day,
Lucky's life changed forever.
Stuffed into the mailbox
was a letter from his Great Aunt
Thelma, addressed to someone
Lucky had never heard of:
a Herbert Morgenstern.

"Who's this?" Lucky asked his
mother.

Mrs. Morgenstern studied the
envelope. "It's *you*," she said.

Thelma Morgenstern
1313 Gray Avenue
Tulsa, Oklahoma

Herbert Morgenstern
9292 Elizabeth Street
New Albany, Indiana

Lucky's mother might as well have said he had four heads, or lived on the moon.

"My name is LUCKY," he said, and laughed.

"Sure, that's your nickname," Mrs. Morgenstern said. "Your grandfather called you that when you were born, and it just stuck." She went to a trunk and fished out a certificate. "But your real name is Herbert."

Lucky's mouth dropped open as he studied the piece of paper: It said someone named Herbert Morgenstern was born on his birthday. It said his mother and father were the parents.

"But—" Lucky said, feeling
quite sick, "you're sure this is me?"
His mother nodded.
And, in that tiniest of seconds,
Lucky *wasn't*.

His mind ran wild, like a
balloon with a hole that whizzed
and looped inside his head.
"I'm not Lucky. . ." he repeated
over and over again.

This was not like when you
pretended to be someone else,
he thought, like an astronaut, or
an explorer. Lucky had discovered
that he *was* someone else. Someone
named Herbert.

"And if my name is not Lucky,"
he gasped, "then I must not *be*
lucky." His life suddenly seemed
like a terrible lie.

"Don't worry about it,
Lucky," his mother said.
"Herbert!" he cried,
"my name is Herbert."
And he refused to answer
to anything else.

From that moment on, ~~Lucky's~~ Herbert's
lucky life became just the opposite.

All around him, life seemed horrible. Weeds snarled as he walked by, flowers wilted, stars clouded over. His parents, his hamster, and especially his little sister were peevish and irritating.

Worst of all was his grandfather: This was all his fault.

"Don't be silly," Grandfather pleaded. "It doesn't matter what your name is. You are still the luckiest kid on the planet."

"Go away," was all Herbert would say.

The more his grandfather insisted that he was lucky, the angrier Herbert became. "So prove it," he snapped. "Name *one* lucky thing about my life."

No matter what his grandfather said, Herbert had an answer. His friends? Stupid. His rock collection? Boring. His hamster? Nothing more than a fuzzy rat.

"Leave me alone," Herbert said.

His grandfather tried to reason with him. "Someday you'll believe it," he said. "Someday you'll think of that *one* thing to prove that you are lucky, after all."

"Go away," Herbert said again.
So at last, his grandfather did.

Life quickly got worse. Every morning,
Herbert woke up saying, "I wonder what terrible
things will happen today?"

"I'll probably get a sunburn," he grumbled
if the sun shone. And if it was raining,
he complained even more, certain
he would lose his umbrella.

No matter what happened,
Herbert blamed it on bad luck.
He went fishing alone, and caught nothing.

He played checkers with himself and lost.

He hated his drawings,

found no rocks for his collection,

crashed his scooter,
and his Razzmatazz-Red crayon was
lost for good. None of it surprised him.

All of this time, Grandfather
watched through the sun and the
rain as Herbert went from bad to
worse. "Soon," he said, "Herbert
will think of that one lucky thing."

At first Herbert's friends tried to cheer him up. He snarled, and huffed and stomped his feet in response. At last they gave up.

Soon no one wanted to sit
next to him, no one wanted to
talk to him—and you can be
sure that no one ever wanted
to borrow his socks.

Still, Grandfather looked on,
day in and day out, certain that
at any second, Herbert would
think of that one lucky thing to
prove that he was lucky after all.

Herbert just wallowed in his
bad luck like a pig in mud.

Then one day
Grandfather was gone.

"He's sick," Mrs. Morgenstern explained on their way to the hospital. "We need you to cheer him up."

Herbert stood beside his grandfather's bed and stared. Grandfather looked so little, lying there asleep.

"I'll be back later," Herbert's mother whispered, and the door closed behind her.

Alone with his grandfather, Herbert suddenly stopped feeling angry and started feeling scared.

What if he was so unlucky that his grandfather didn't get better?

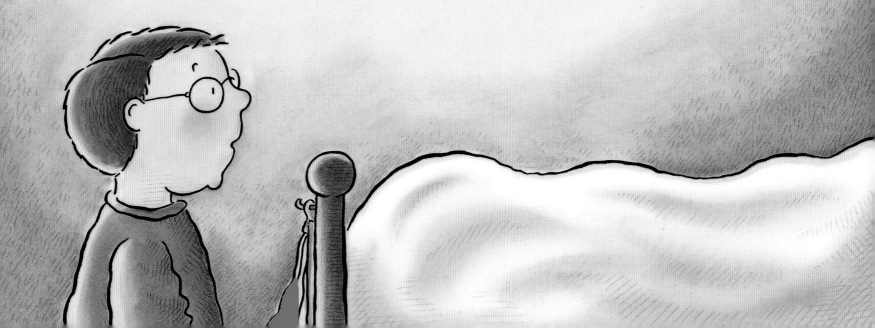

Oh, how Herbert wished
he had never argued with
his grandfather, how he
longed for the days when
he was still Lucky!

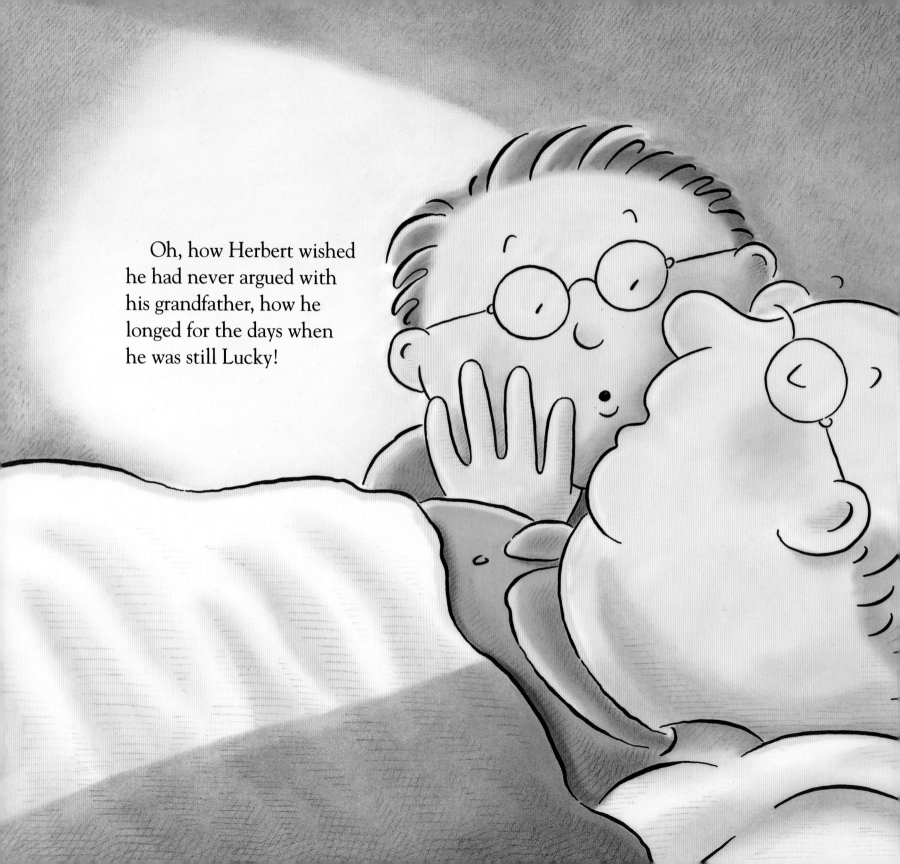

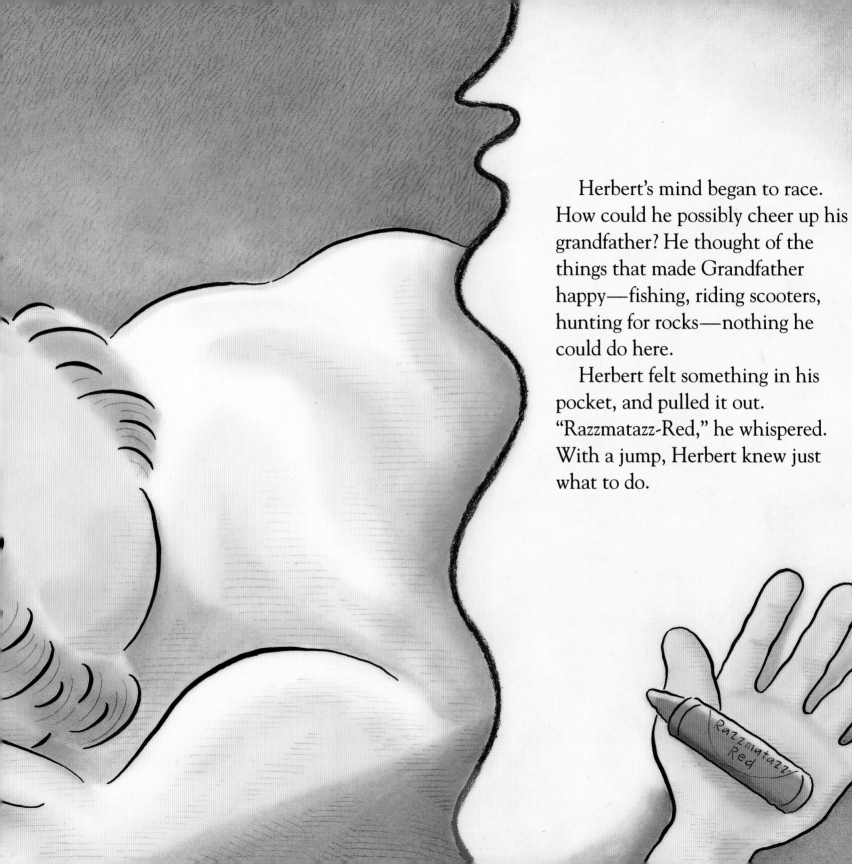

Herbert's mind began to race. How could he possibly cheer up his grandfather? He thought of the things that made Grandfather happy—fishing, riding scooters, hunting for rocks—nothing he could do here.

Herbert felt something in his pocket, and pulled it out. "Razzmatazz-Red," he whispered. With a jump, Herbert knew just what to do.

Pulling some paper from the nurse's
charts, Herbert began to draw. He drew
himself and his grandfather fishing and riding
scooters, playing chess, and baking cookies. . .
One drawing led to the next, and the next.

Each drawing was hung on the wall, until at last Herbert stood back. "Someday," he remembered his grandfather saying, "you'll think of that *one* thing to prove that you are lucky, after all."

And in that very instant Herbert finally saw it, right there in front of him: his *one lucky thing*.

By the time Grandfather woke up, his room was a magical sea of drawings.

"Grandfather!" Herbert shouted. "I thought of it, just like you said I would—I thought of that one thing to prōve that I am lucky, after all."

Grandfather blinked his eyes and smiled at the drawings. "That big fish you caught?" he asked, pointing. Herbert shook his head no.

"All the chess games you won?" No again.

"The rocks you found, your hamster, your Razzmatazz-Red crayon?" Grandfather listed everything he saw in the drawings. All no's. "What then?" he asked, bewildered. "What could it be?"

"It's what is in all of the drawings," Herbert said. "My lucky thing is *you*."

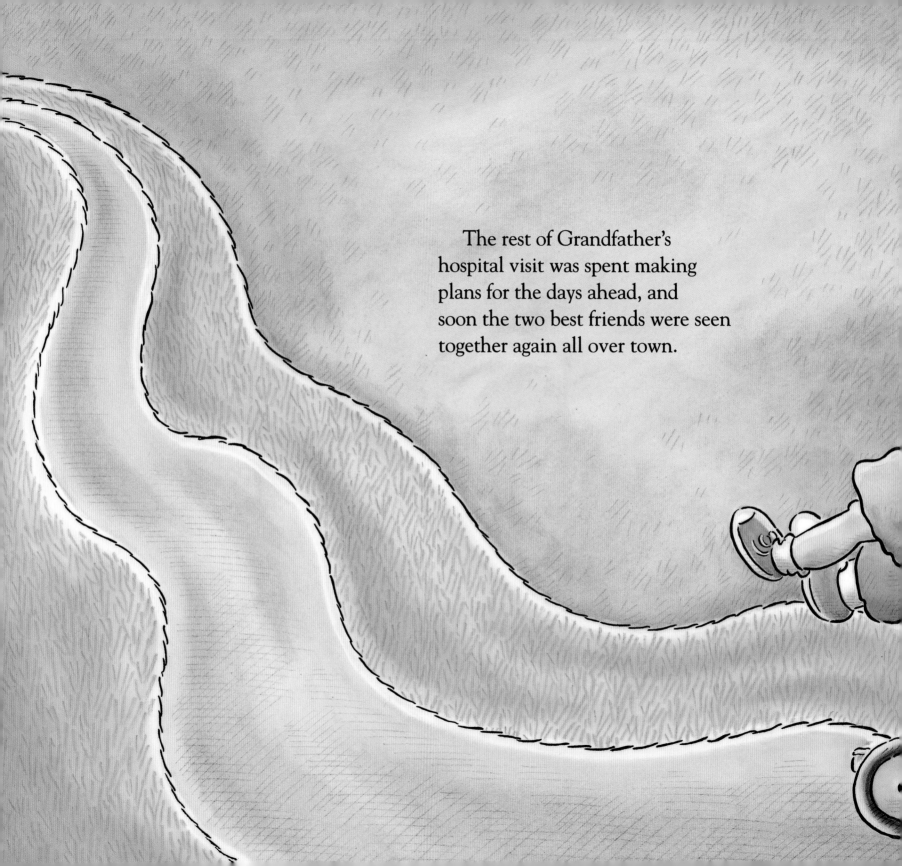

The rest of Grandfather's
hospital visit was spent making
plans for the days ahead, and
soon the two best friends were seen
together again all over town.

"Herbert, my boy,"
Grandfather could often be
overheard saying, "*we* are
the luckiest kids on the planet."
And Herbert, of course, was
always quick to agree.

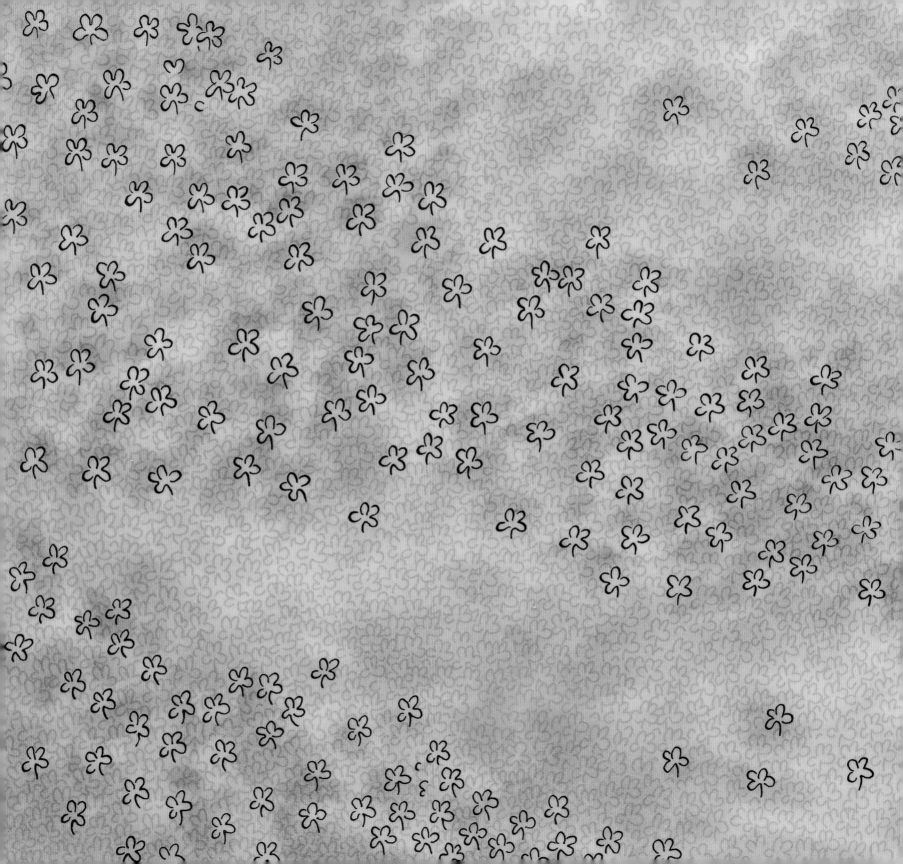